Farmyard Tales Flip Books
The Runaway Tractor

Heather Amery

Illustrated by Stephen Cartwright

Language consultant: Betty Root
Series editor: Jenny Tyler

There is a little yellow duck to find on every page.

This is Apple Tree Farm.

This is Mrs. Boot, the farmer. She has two children, called Poppy and Sam, and a dog called Rusty.

Ted is the tractor driver.

He has filled the trailer with hay. He is taking it to the fields to feed the sheep.

Poppy and Sam hear a funny noise.

"Listen," says Sam. "Ted is shouting and the
tractor is making a funny noise. Let's go and look."

They run to the top of the hill.

The tractor is racing down the hill, going faster and faster. "It won't stop," shouts Ted.

The trailer comes off.

The trailer runs down the hill and crashes into a fence. It tips up and all the hay falls out.

The tractor runs into the pond.

The tractor hits the water with a great splash. The engine makes a loud noise, then it stops with a hiss.

Ted climbs down from the tractor.

Ted paddles through the water and out of the pond. Poppy and Sam run down the hill.

Ted is very wet.

Ted takes off his boots and tips out the water.
How can he get the tractor out of the pond?

"Go and ask Farmer Dray to help."

"Ask someone to telephone Farmer Dray," says Ted.
Poppy and Sam run off to the house.

Farmer Dray has a big horse.

Soon he walks down the hill with his horse.
It is a huge carthorse, called Dolly.

Ted helps with the ropes.

Farmer Dray ties the ropes to the horse. Ted ties the other ends to the tractor.

Dolly pulls and pulls.

Very slowly the tractor starts to move. Ted
pushes as hard as he can and Dolly pulls.

Ted falls over.

The tractor jerks forward and Ted falls in the water. Now he is wet and muddy all over.

The tractor is out of the pond.

"Better leave the tractor to dry," says Farmer Dray. "Then you can get the engine going again."

Poppy and Sam ride home.

Farmer Dray lifts them onto Dolly's back.
But Ted is so muddy, he has to walk.

"Thank you very much."

They wave as the balloon takes off again.
"We were flying," says Sam.

"We're going down now," says Tim.

The balloon floats down and the basket lands in a field. Mrs. Boot helps Poppy and Sam out.

The balloon floats along.

"I can see our farm down there," says Poppy.
"Look, there's Alice in the truck," says Sam.

The balloon goes up.

Slowly it leaves the ground. Tim turns off the burner. "The wind is blowing us along," he says.

Mrs. Boot, Poppy and Sam climb in.

Tim lights the gas burner. The big flames make
a loud noise. "Hold on tight," says Alice.

"Would you like a ride?"

"Oh, yes please," says Poppy. "Just a little one," says Tim. "The truck will bring you back."

They blow up the balloon.

Poppy and Sam help Tim hold open the balloon.
A fan blows hot air into it. It gets bigger and bigger.

Alice helps to unload the truck.

Tim unloads the empty cylinders. Then he puts the new ones into the balloon's basket.

"A truck is following us."

"There it is now," says Alice. "Our friend is bringing more cylinders of gas for the balloon."

The man climbs out.

"I'm Alice and this is Tim," says the woman.
"We ran out of gas. Sorry about your cows."

There are two people in it.

"Where are we?" asks the man. "This is Apple Tree Farm. You frightened our cows," says Mrs. Boot.

"It's a hot air balloon."

"It's coming down," says Mrs. Boot. "It's going to land in our field." The balloon hits the ground.

They all run out to the field.

The cows are running around the field. They are scared. A big balloon is floating over the trees.

Today is Saturday.

Mrs. Boot, Poppy and Sam are having breakfast.
"Why are the cows so noisy?" asks Sam.

This is Apple Tree Farm.

This is Mrs. Boot, the farmer. She has two children, called Poppy and Sam, and a dog called Rusty.

Farmyard Tales Flip Books

Surprise Visitors

Heather Amery

Illustrated by Stephen Cartwright

Language consultant: Betty Root
Series editor: Jenny Tyler

There is a little yellow duck to find on every page.